OUTSIDE AND INSIDE
BIG CATS
BY SANDRA MARKLE

ATHENEUM BOOKS FOR YOUNG READERS

NEW YORK   LONDON   TORONTO   SYDNEY   SINGAPORE

Look at this cougar chasing a snowshoe hare. Do you ever wonder why cats are such good hunters—even if it's only a house cat stalking a toy mouse? This book will help you take a closer look at cats—outside and inside—and find out.

Do you have a lion living in your house? Probably not, but a lion is just a scaled-up house cat. Whatever size a cat is, it spends a lot of time doing nothing—or so it seems. In fact most cats sleep from thirteen to eighteen hours a day. This lets them save their energy for the bursts of activity needed to hunt and catch food.

Even when they're awake, cats may seem to be resting. Oftentimes, they're hiding from enemies or stalking *prey*. In the wild, a cat's fur coat is just the right color to let it stay safely out of sight. The panther's black coat makes it stand out during the day. But at night when it's hunting, the panther can easily slip through the dark without being noticed.

Like splotches of light and shadow, this leopard family's spots help them hide while they eat. Spots or stripes break up a cat's solid shape, making the animal harder to pick out from its surroundings.

A cat's fur coat also helps it stay warm and dry. Like wearing long underwear under a sweater, most cats have longer outer hairs to shed water, and a short undercoat to trap body heat.

If a cat's ever licked you, you know its *tongue* feels rough. That's because a cat's tongue is covered with spines. That makes a cat's tongue a good comb, so licking rakes away dirt and smoothes out hair. Licking also spreads the oil that's naturally produced in the cat's skin. This helps to waterproof its fur coat.

Licking one another lets cats groom hard-to-reach places. It's also their way of being part of a family. So mother cats groom their kittens, and cats living together, like a group of lions, groom one another.

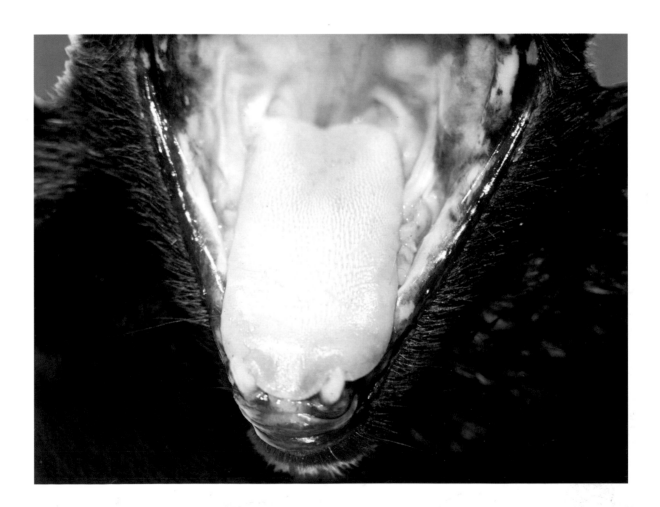

A cat's tongue has another important job: carrying water to its mouth. Like yours, a cat's body needs water to function. Some of that water, though, comes from eating moist food, like a juicy antelope.

Look at this jaguar's *whiskers*—the stiff hairs sticking out above the cat's eyes, at the back of its cheeks, and on either side of its nose. When touched, they send signals to the cat's *brain*. Once the brain interprets these messages, the cat knows how close things are around it. So a hunting cat senses where it can squeeze through thick brush even in the dark. When it pounces on its prey, a cat pulls its whiskers forward to help judge when to sink in its *teeth.*

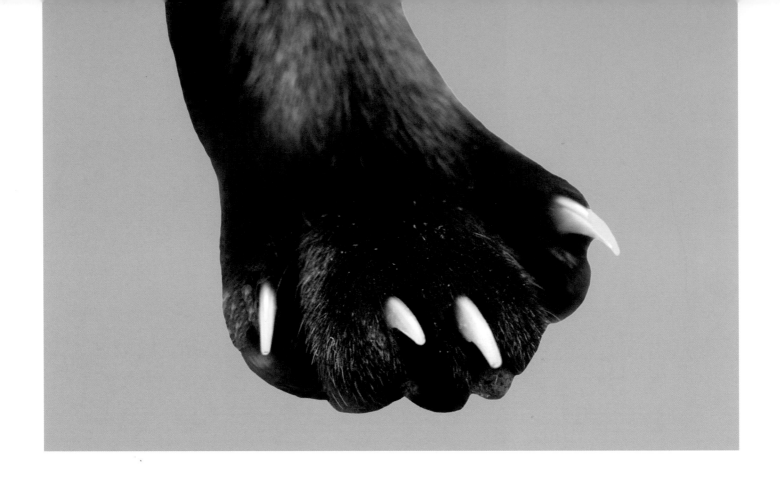

Feel your fingernails. A cat's *claws* are made of this same tough, flexible material. Like your fingernails, a cat's claws keep on growing, replacing what's worn away.

Cats count on their sharp claws to catch prey, but they walk and run on their toes. So the claws need protection to stay sharp. Imagine being able to bend just the tips of your toes up and backward! Luckily most cats can do this.

When the tips of a cat's toes are relaxed, an elastic band retracts the claws into its furry paws. When the cat wants to push its claws out, it rotates the tips of its toes, thrusting them out.

Unlike other cats a cheetah's claws aren't covered and don't fully retract—but for a cheetah, that's good. Cheetahs need their claws to dig in when they're chasing down prey. For short bursts, a cheetah can run as fast as 70 miles (112 kilometers) per hour—about the speed a car can drive on an expressway. So a cheetah's strong claws and rough paw pads keep the cat from slipping as it twists and turns.

Lions aren't as fast as cheetahs. So this lion slipped up close to its prey before bursting out of the long grass. Once the lion pounced, it pulled the tips of its toes down, the way you would move your fingers to make a fist. This anchored the lion's claws in the prey's neck. The lion could then easily hang on while it made its kill.

This tiger is spraying the tree with urine. The big cat isn't just getting rid of wastes. It's marking the tree with its own personal smell.

All cats claim a *home range*—even house cats claim their house. To make sure their claim is clear, cats may leave their feces, called scat. Or they may scratch a tree or furniture. This also leaves behind some of their smell, because cats have scent glands in their paws. Cats usually don't share their home range with another cat of the same sex. A male, though, is likely to overlap the ranges of several females.

Look at this lion biting a zebra. Besides its claws, a cat counts on its teeth to catch prey. See the lion's long teeth? They're called fangs, or canine teeth. The lion sinks these teeth deep into its prey's throat to make the kill. Run your tongue around your teeth. Feel the four pointed teeth—two above and two below. A cat's teeth are all sharp and pointed like that. So once its food is caught, a cat uses its teeth to slice off chunks of food.

This leopard moved the warthog it killed into a tree because bigger cats or other animals, like hyenas, may try to steal its food. Did you know that the leopard carried the warthog in its jaws? Imagine what it would be like to have to carry everything you move, in your mouth!

A mother cougar's jaws are strong enough to kill and carry a prey nearly as big as she is. Like all cats though, she can control how hard she bites. Here, a mother cougar carries her baby so gently, her teeth won't even scratch his skin.

Look at the cheetah's flat face. Its short, domed head and large nose openings let it quickly inhale a lot of air—just what it needs to run fast and catch prey without running out of breath. Once it catches its prey, it next makes the kill. With small animals, like hares, the cheetah bites through the prey's skull. With large animals, like zebras, it suffocates its prey by clamping its mouth over the animal's throat, sometimes for as long as five minutes.

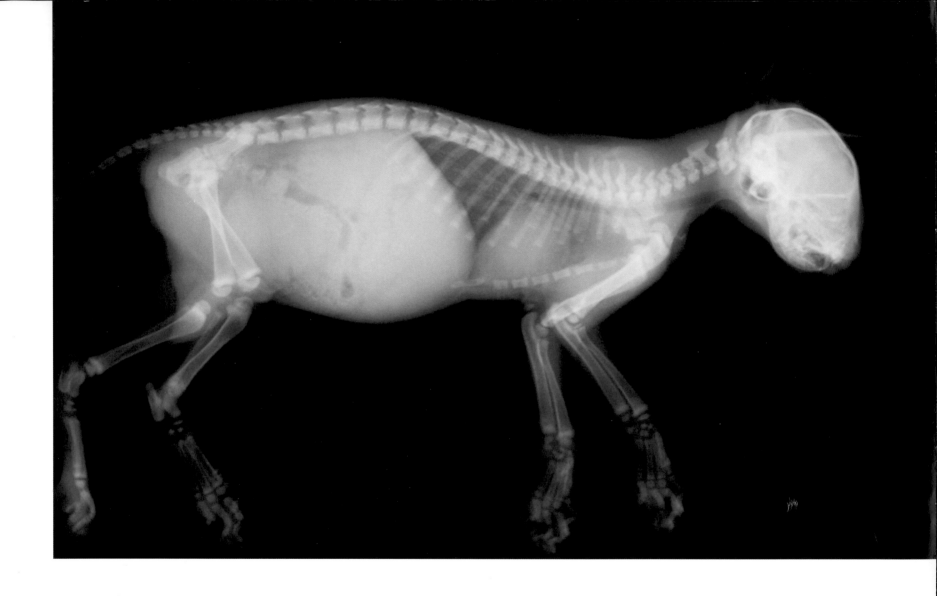

So what's inside a cat's body to help it do all it does? *Bones,* for one thing.

Squeeze your arm and pat your knees to feel the bones inside. Like you, a cat has a hard, bony inside framework, or *skeleton*, that gives its body shape. Now bend your fingers, arms, and legs. Like you, a cat can only bend where bones meet. A cat's back is made up of many small bones shaped to slide easily over one another. That makes a cat's back very flexible—just right for twisting and turning during a chase or curling up in a ball for a nap.

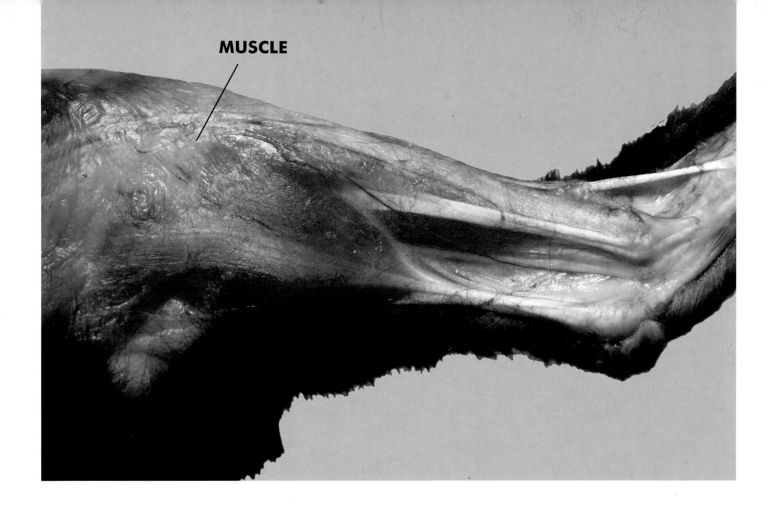

MUSCLE

Now bend your leg and squeeze your calf. The bulge you feel is *muscle.* Like yours, a cat's body would not be able to move without muscles to pull on bones. A cat's hind leg bones and muscles work together to help it jump. To get ready to jump, a cat crouches, pushing the heels of its hind legs to the ground. This stretches strong bands holding the bones and muscles together. Like releasing a stretched rubber band, these bands and the muscles launch a jumping cat forward and upward. Many cats can jump as much as ten times their length! You can probably only jump about half your height.

This female lion and her offspring have just caught their dinner. Lions live in groups called *prides.* The females of the pride work together when they hunt to separate a prey animal from a herd and catch it. Older cubs are in training and often take part in the hunt. The male lion is bigger than the female, and his bushy mane makes it hard for him to sneak up on prey. He usually only joins the hunt when the pride attacks really big prey, such as a water buffalo.

See how this cougar's ears are aimed in two different directions? Muscles let a cat move its ears separately to pinpoint sounds. The cougar's cup-shaped ears pick up sound waves and direct them to the inner ear. From there, signals are sent to the brain. Once the brain interprets these messages, the cat hears. Cats can hear a wide range of sounds—even high-pitched mouse squeaks that you probably wouldn't even notice.

This lioness is making a really big sound—a roar. Cats make a lot of different sounds, but only four kinds of cats can roar: lions, tigers, leopards, and jaguars. These cats have an elastic cord connecting their tongue to thick vocal cords and a flexible voice box. When the cat forces air through this voice system, it produces a loud, booming roar. So why do cats roar? They may do it to claim a home range and find a mate. Or sometimes, like the lioness, they roar just because they want to.

Take a close look at this tiger's eyes. Like yours, a cat's eyes face forward, letting both eyes work together. This lets a cat judge how far it has to run or jump to catch its prey. Light reflected from objects enters the eyes through pupils, openings that look like dark spots. When this light strikes the layer of cells, called the *retina*, at the back of the eyes, signals are sent to the brain. Once the brain interprets these signals, the cat is able to see.

The lions' eyes seem to glow in the dark. That glow is actually light reflecting off a mirrorlike layer behind the retina. This layer bounces the light that passed through the retina back through it again. So the retina's light-sensing cells get a second chance to send signals to the brain. While this doesn't give cats the ability to see in total darkness, it lets them see in much dimmer light than you can.

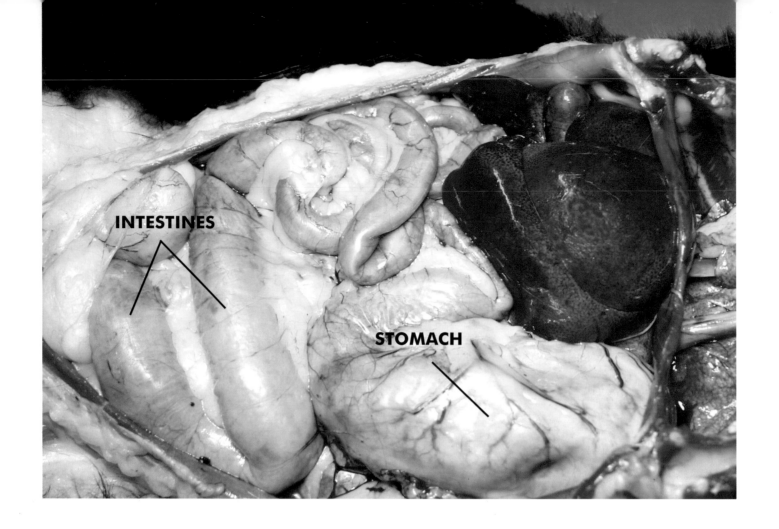

INTESTINES

STOMACH

Once cats catch their prey, they gulp down skin, muscles, guts, and even small bones. They don't chew their food very well, so their digestive system has to break it down. This job starts in the *stomach*. There, special juices break the food into its chemical building blocks, called *nutrients.*

In the *intestine,* the food nutrients pass into the bloodstream and are carried to all parts of the body. After you eat, it takes your body more than a day to pass solid wastes. A cat's intestine is shorter than yours, so food wastes are passed much faster. Because wastes add weight, this helps a cat stay light enough to run away if it needs to escape enemies.

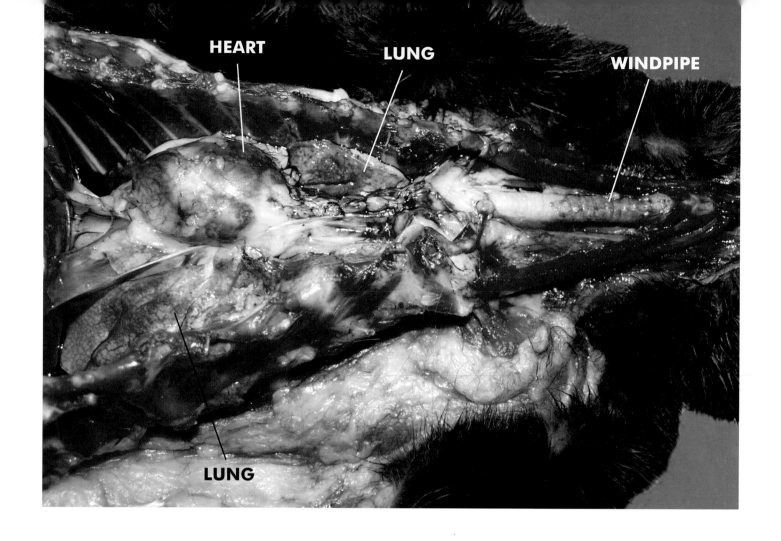

HEART   LUNG   WINDPIPE

LUNG

To get the energy it needs to be active, stay warm, and grow, a cat must have a steady supply of *oxygen.* Oxygen combines with food nutrients to release energy. A cat gets oxygen by breathing in air. The air flows down the *windpipe* into the *lungs.* There, oxygen is exchanged for the waste gas, *carbon dioxide.* The cat then breathes out this waste gas.

Blood carries the supply of oxygen and food nutrients throughout the cat's body. The *heart* pushes the blood through the body. The heart is a muscle, but a cat does not control its heartbeat the way it does its muscles for running and jumping. The heart has a built-in pacemaker that keeps it beating. The brain controls how fast or slow the heart pumps—fast when the cat is active, slow when it is sleeping.

This male tiger may look like he's growling, but he's really checking if a nearby female is ready to mate. He does this by detecting her scent. You detect a scent when chemical bits, carried by the air, trigger sensors inside your nose. These send messages to your brain, and once your brain interprets the messages, you become aware of the scent. Cats detect scents this way, too, but they also have other smell sensors inside their mouth—sensors you don't have.

By pressing the middle of its tongue to the roof of its mouth, the tiger is carrying airborne droplets of urine deposited by the female to its special sensors. When its brain interprets these messages, the male knows if the female tiger is ready to mate.

Whenever cats mate, a cell from the male, called a *sperm* cell, joins with the female's *egg* cell. Then the young, or *embryos,* develop inside the mother's body. Each embryo is attached to its mother by a special cord, and through this, it receives the food nutrients and oxygen it needs to grow. This is the way you developed, too, but it took nine months before you were ready to be born. Most kittens are born in just three months. This mother cougar is cleaning one cub while another nurses, sucking milk from one of her nipples.

All the cubs in a lion pride are born at about the same time. Then the mothers share the job of raising the woolly cubs. The cubs are allowed to nurse from any mother, so one with fewer cubs can help others with more. All lion cubs are about the same size, so there isn't one big cub hogging all the milk. Male lions and adult females without cubs help, too, keeping the cubs safe from enemies, like hyenas, until the youngsters grow big enough to take care of themselves.

This young leopard is a hunter in training. Its mother killed this impala. Now it's practicing how to drag prey with the least effort. Young hunters may also need help tearing apart a meal until they get their adult teeth.

These young cougars must still depend on their mother for food, but they're already learning about the world around them. They're discovering the sounds, smells, and sights that will help them find prey. Soon they'll be grown up, and each young cougar will leave the family group to hunt alone.

Now you know why cats are able to be such good hunters. Their bodies are designed for this way of life from the inside out.

Glossary and Index

Note: Glossary words are italicized the first time they appear in text.

BONES bōnz: The hard but lightweight parts that form the body's supporting frame. **20, 21, 23, 30**

BRAIN brān: Body part that receives the messages about what is happening inside and outside the body. It sends messages to put the body into action. **11, 25, 28, 32, 33**

CARBON DIOXIDE 'kär-bən dī-'äk-sīd: A gas that is given off naturally in body activities, carried to the lungs by the blood, and breathed out. **31**

CLAW klaw: Hard, sharp body part on the toes used for getting food and climbing. **12, 13, 14, 16**

EGG eg: Female reproductive cell. **34**

EMBRYO em'-brē-ō: Name given to the young developing in the womb. **34**

HEART härt: Body part that acts like a pump, constantly pushing blood throughout the cat's body. **31, 32**

HOME RANGE hōm rānj: The area within which the lion pride usually hunts. **15, 27**

INTESTINE in-tes'-tin: The tube-shaped body part where food is mixed with special digestive juices to break it down into nutrients. The nutrients then pass through the walls of the intestine, into the bloodstream. **30**

LUNG ləng: Body part where oxygen and carbon dioxide are exchanged. **31**

MUSCLES məs'-əlz: Working in pairs, muscles move the cat's bones by pulling on them. **23, 25, 30, 32**

NUTRIENTS nü-trē-əntz: Chemical building blocks into which food is broken down for use by the cat's body. The five basic nutrients provided by food are proteins, fats, carbohydrates, minerals, and vitamins. **30, 31, 32, 34**

OXYGEN ok'-si-jən: A gas in the air that is breathed into the lungs, carried by the blood throughout the body, and combined with food nutrients to release energy. **31, 32, 34**

PREY prā: An animal hunted by a cat. **6, 11, 12, 13, 14, 16, 18, 19, 24, 28, 30, 36, 37**

PRIDE prīd: A group of lions that lives and hunts together. **24, 35**

RETINA 'ret-nə: Layer at the back of the eye that is made up of light-sensitive cells. When light strikes the cells, messages are sent to the brain. Once the brain interprets these messages, a cat sees. **28, 29**

SKELETON skel'-ə-tən: The framework of bones that supports the body and gives it its shape. **20, 21**

SPERM spurm: The male reproductive cell. **34**

STOMACH stəm'-ək: Tubelike body part where bacteria break down much of the plant material before it is passed into the small intestine. **30**

TOOTH 'tüth: Sharp, hard part in the mouth used for biting into food. In cats, it's shaped for slicing. **11, 16, 18, 36**

TONGUE təng: A bundle of movable muscles attached to the floor of the mouth. The cat uses its tongue to clean itself, to peel meat off bone, and to bring food and water into its mouth. **9, 10, 27, 33**

WHISKER 'wis-kər: Special body hair that sticks out from around a cat's face, helping it judge how close it is to things around it. **11**

WINDPIPE 'win-pīp: Tube that carries air from the nose and mouth to the lungs and back out again. **31**

Looking Back

1. Take another look at the black panther on page 6 and the leopards on page 7. You may be surprised to learn that a black panther is a leopard with a black coat. In fact, black panthers have darker black spots, which you can only see in bright sunlight.

2. Take a close look at the tiger on page 10. Notice how his ears are turned to listen behind him while he's drinking.

3. Find a picture in the book that shows how having a flexible back helps cats.

4. Look closely on page 34 at the cougar babies with their mother. How do you think being spotted may help keep them safe?

5. Look back on page 22 at the jumping tiger. Did you guess that this cat's long tail helps it keep its balance?

6. The photograph of the roaring lion mother on page 26 gives you another chance to check out a cat's teeth. Because a cat's teeth are all sharp, when a cat bites, its teeth act like scissors, snipping off food.

Photo Credits

Cover: Tom and Pat Leeson, Leeson Photo
Title Page: Erwin and Peggy Bauer
p. 2 Erwin and Peggy Bauer
p. 4 Rich Kirchner
p. 5 Skip Jeffery
p. 6 Erwin and Peggy Bauer
p. 7 Erwin and Peggy Bauer
p. 8 Rich Kirchner
p. 9 Skip Jeffery
p. 10 Tom and Pat Leeson, Leeson Photo
p. 11 Erwin and Peggy Bauer
p. 12 Skip Jeffery
p. 13 Minden Photos/Iwago
p. 14 Rich Kirchner
p. 15 Tom and Pat Leeson, Leeson Photo
p. 16 Minden Photos/Iwago
p. 17 Rich Kirchner
p. 18 Erwin and Peggy Bauer
p. 19 Tom and Pat Leeson, Leeson Photo
p. 20 Anthony Mitchell
p. 21 Rich Kirchner
p. 22 Minden Photos/Tim Fitzharris
p. 23 Skip Jeffery
p. 24 Erwin and Peggy Bauer
p. 25 Erwin and Peggy Bauer
p. 26 Animals Animals/Gerard Lacz
p. 28 Tom and Pat Leeson, Leeson Photo
p. 29 Minden Photos/Frans Lanting
p. 30 Skip Jeffery
p. 31 Skip Jeffery
p. 32 Rich Kirchner
p. 33 Tom and Pat Leeson, Leeson Photo
p. 34 Rich Kirchner
p. 35 Rich Kirchner
p. 36 Erwin and Peggy Bauer
p. 37 Tom and Pat Leeson, Leeson Photo

With love, for dear friends John and Barbara Clampet

The author would like to thank the following for sharing their expertise and enthusiasm:
Dr. Douglas L. Armstrong, D.V.M., Veterinarian, Henry Doorly Zoo, Omaha, Nebraska;
Dr. Thomas G. Curro, D.V.M., M.S., Associate Veterinarian, Henry Doorly Zoo, Omaha, Nebraska;
and Dr. Jill Mellen, Research Biologist at Disney's Animal Kingdom. And a special thanks to Skip Jeffery
for his help and support.

ATHENEUM BOOKS FOR YOUNG READERS
An imprint of Simon & Schuster Children's Publishing Division
1230 Avenue of the Americas
New York, New York 10020
Text copyright © 2003 by Sandra Markle
The text of this book is set in Melior.
Manufactured in China
First Edition
2 4 6 8 10 9 7 5 3 1
Library of Congress Cataloging-in-Publication Data
Markle, Sandra.
Outside and inside big cats / by Sandra Markle.—1st ed.
p. cm.
Summary: Focuses on big cats such as lions, tigers, jaguars, and cougars.
ISBN 0-689-82299-5
1.Felidae—Juvenile literature. [1. Cat family (Mammals)] I. Title.
QL737.C23 M273 2002
599.75—dc21
2001046368